W9-CDZ-699

MAPLE RIDGE

LOGAN PRYCE MAKES A MESS

By Grace Gilmore
Illustrated by Petra Brown

LITTLE SIMON
NEW YORK LONDON TORONTO SYDNEY NEW DELHI

I want to thank my wonderful editor, Sonali Fry.

I also want to thank the History Center in Tompkins County for their invaluable assistance in my research.

— G. G.

LITTLE SIMON
An imprint of Simon & Schuster Children's Publishing Division
1230 Avenue of the Americas, New York, New York 10020
This Little Simon edition April 2015

For information about special discounts for bulk purchases, please contact Simon & Schuster Special Sales at 1-866-506-1949 or business@simonandschuster.com.
The Simon & Schuster Speakers Bureau can bring authors to your live event. For more information or to book an event, contact the Simon & Schuster Speakers Bureau at 1-866-248-3049 or visit our website at www.simonspeakers.com.
Designed by Chani Yammer
The illustrations for this book were rendered in pen and ink.
The text of this book was set in Caecilia.
Manufactured in the United States of America 0315 FFG
10 9 8 7 6 5 4 3 2 1
Library of Congress Cataloging-in-Publication Data
Gilmore, Grace. Logan Pryce makes a mess / by Grace Gilmore ;
illustrated by Petra Brown. —First edition. pages cm. — (Tales from Maple Ridge ;
1) Summary: "When his father is hired for a temporary job at the general store, farm boy Logan can't wait to lend a hand. But his eagerness may cause his dad to lose this job. Can Logan's mistake be fixed in time?"
— Provided by publisher. ISBN 978-1-4814-2624-4 (pbk : alk. paper) —
ISBN 978-1-4814-2625-1 (hc : alk. paper) — ISBN 978-1-4814-2626-8 (ebook)
[1. Family life—Fiction. 2. Farm life—Fiction.] I. Brown, Petra, illustrator. II. Title. PZ7.G4372Lo
2015 [Fic]—dc23 2014005957

CONTENTS

THE FIX-IT SHOP

Logan Pryce picked up a hammer and pounded the tin cup.

"The Fox-Away is going to be my best invention ever," he told Skeeter. Skeeter barked and wagged his honey-colored tail. He always agreed with everything Logan said.

Logan leaned closer to the oil lamp and continued hammering.

Nearby, the horses munched on their oats and paid no attention. The cows did the same with their hay. The farm animals were well used to Logan and his Fix-It Shop.

The Fix-It Shop was where Logan

mended broken things. Sometimes, he even recycled them into new things, like the Fox-Away.

The Fix-It Shop took up an entire stall in the corner of the barn. Logan's worktable was a wooden

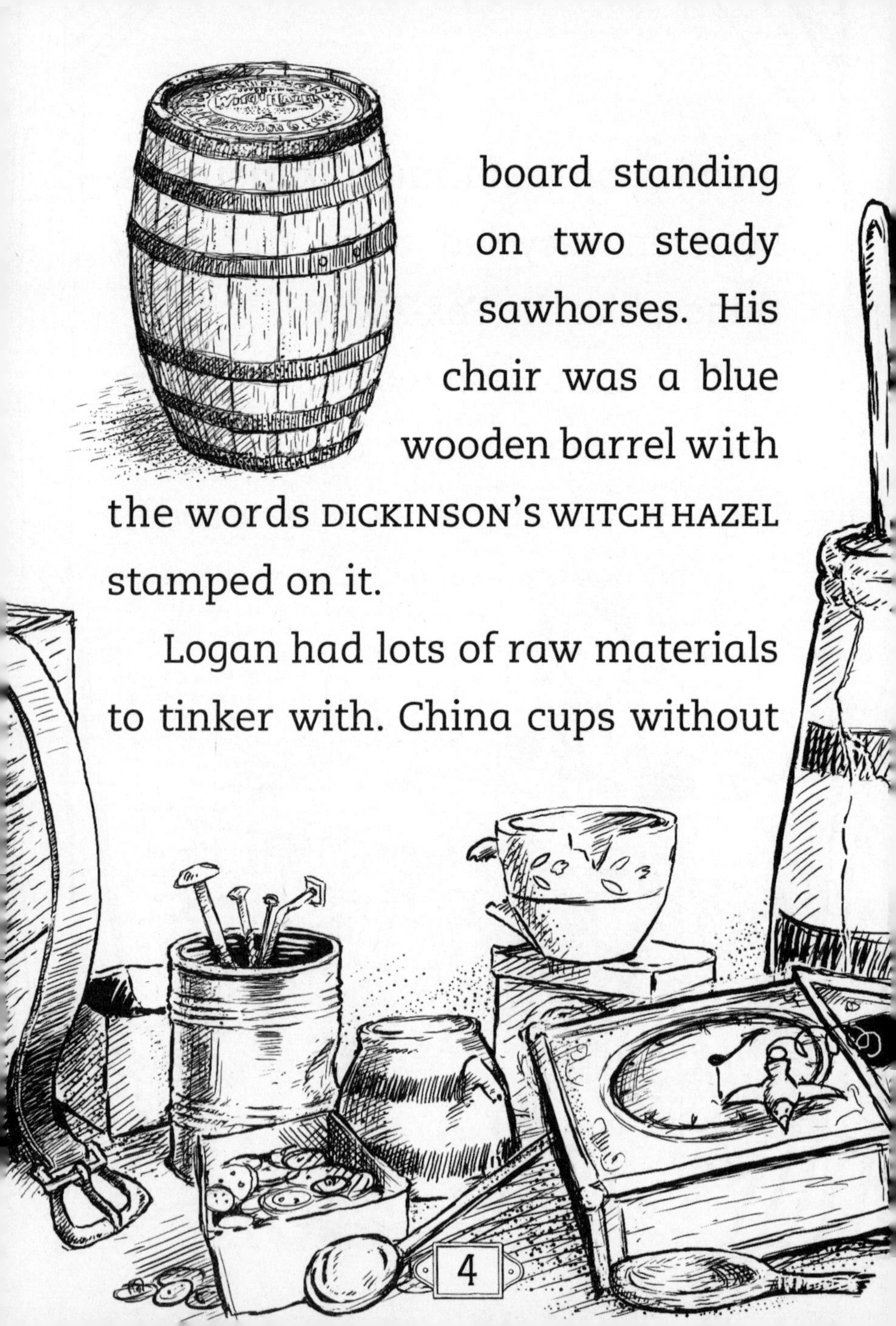

board standing on two steady sawhorses. His chair was a blue wooden barrel with the words DICKINSON'S WITCH HAZEL stamped on it.

Logan had lots of raw materials to tinker with. China cups without

handles. Mismatched buttons. A cracked butter churn. A cuckoo clock that no longer told the time. The objects spilled out of crates and scattered across the floor.

He had many tools, too. His favorite was a silver pocketknife

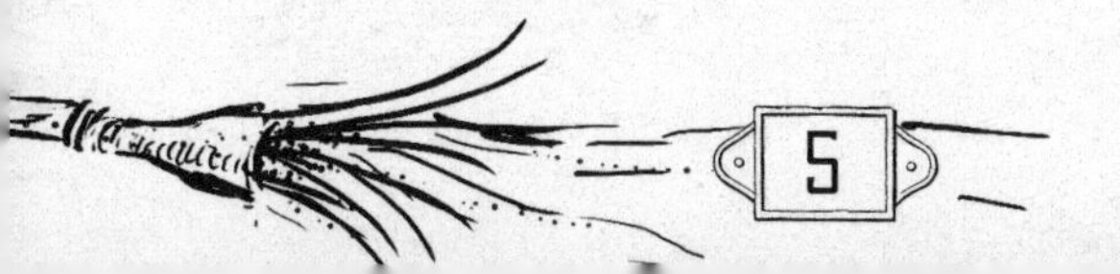

engraved with a maple leaf design. His father had bought it for him at Mayberry's General Store.

The barn doors creaked open. A breeze whooshed in, smelling of earth and early spring. The oil lamp flickered for a moment and then grew still. A cat skittered out from behind one haystack and into another.

"Logan!" His sister Tess stood in the deep shadow of the doorway. "Ma says you need to come in for supper!"

Tess was nine, a year older than Logan. She had hazel eyes and two long brown braids that hung down her shoulders.

"Be there in a minute," said Logan as he reached for a messy ball of twine.

“I think she and Pa want to talk to us.” Tess sounded worried.

“About what?”

“I don’t know. It sounded really important, so let’s get going!”

“Okay, okay.”

Logan scooped up the twine and the tin cup and stuffed them into a gunnysack. He added some other items and blew out the lamp.

He wondered why Ma and Pa wanted to talk to them. Was it about school? Or their chores? Logan *had* knocked over a bucket of fresh milk this morning. But he'd had a good excuse. The bucket had been in the way as he chased a couple of hens that had escaped from the henhouse.

Outside, the sky was big and pink with twilight, and the ground was soft and wet. Logan's boots made squishy noises and splattered mud as he walked. Tess stepped more carefully. Skeeter dashed off to chase a hare into a bush.

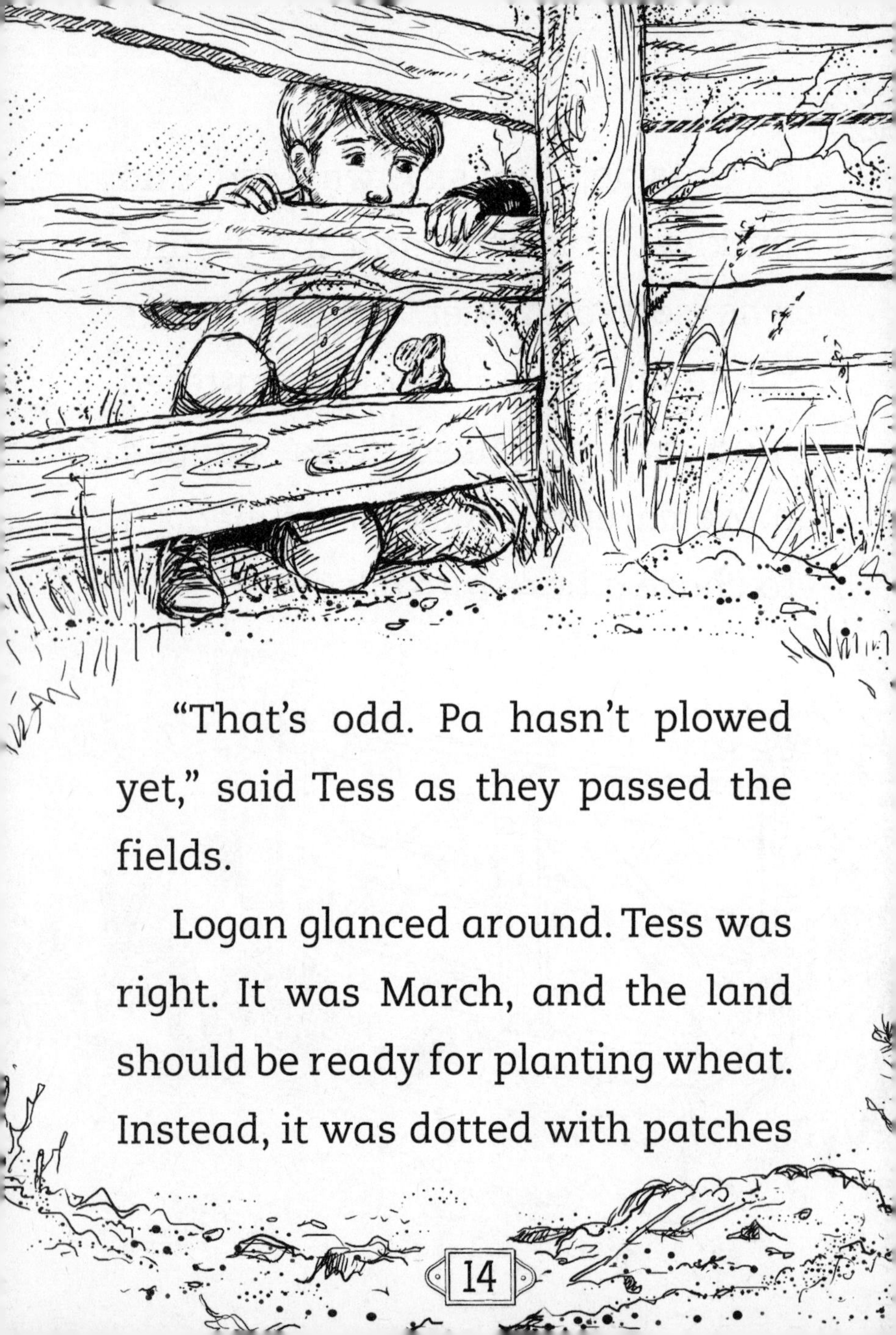

“That’s odd. Pa hasn’t plowed yet,” said Tess as they passed the fields.

Logan glanced around. Tess was right. It was March, and the land should be ready for planting wheat. Instead, it was dotted with patches

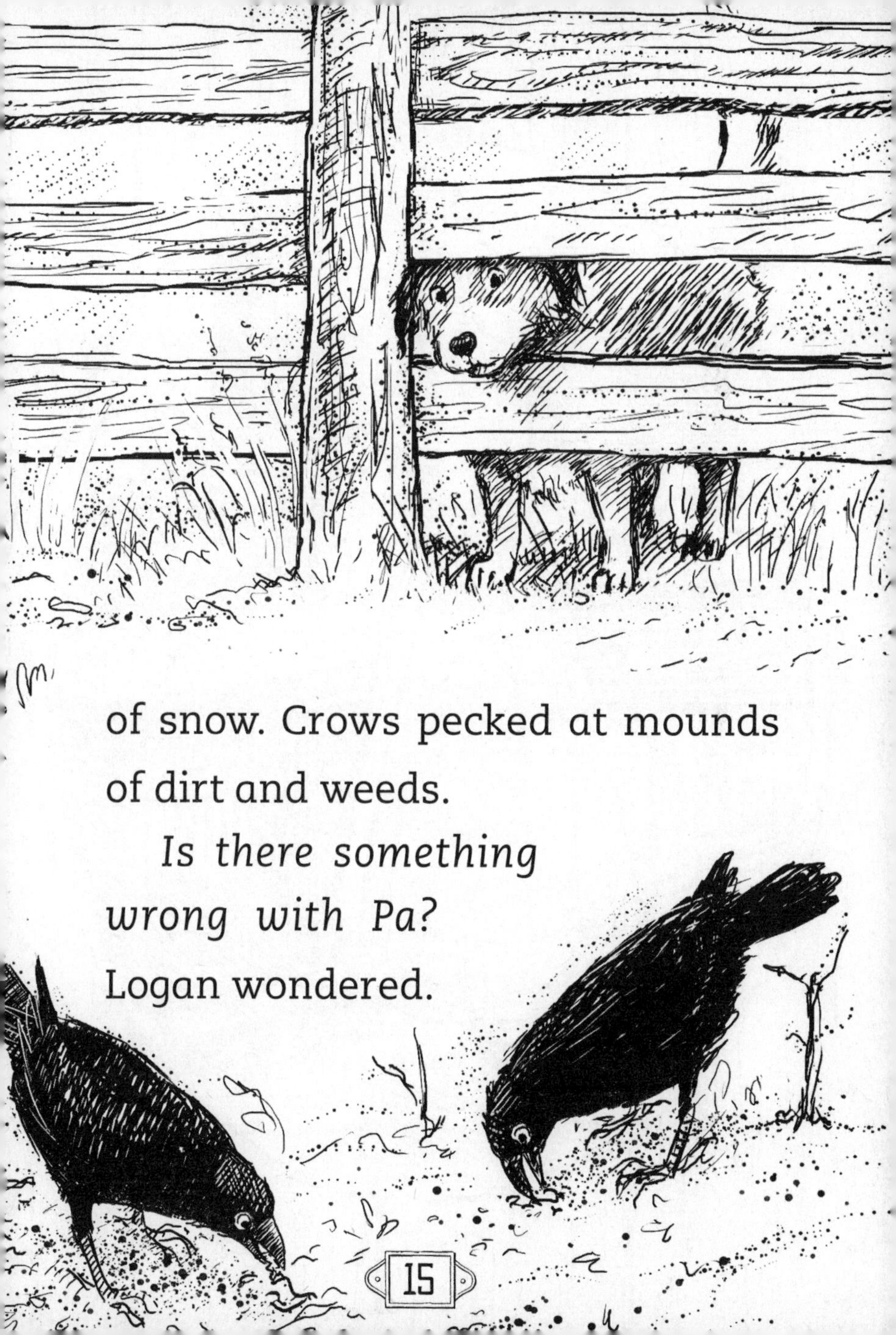

of snow. Crows pecked at mounds of dirt and weeds.

Is there something wrong with Pa? Logan wondered.

NEWS

In the kitchen, Ma stirred a pot of stew at the cast-iron stove. The stove did everything from cooking their food to heating their house. Pa drew water from the indoor pump. The pitcher overflowed into the gray soapstone sink.

"Shoes!" Ma called out as Logan and Tess came in. She frowned

sternly at Logan's mud-covered boots.

Logan unlaced his boots and pulled them off. Tess did the same.

Drew and Annie were sitting at the table. Drew, who was eleven, was adding sums in a notebook.

Annie, who was four, was building a tower out of pickles.

Logan sat down and pulled a doll out of his gunnysack. He brushed hay from its hair and handed it to Annie.

"I fixed her leg," he said.

"Thank you, Lolo!" Annie hugged her doll, which Ma had sewn for her out of fabric scraps. "Are you hungry, Mrs. Wigglesworth? Would you like a pickle?"

Pa and Ma sat down too. Pa poured water into glasses. Ma ladled stew into bowls and passed around a plate of warm biscuits. Skeeter's eyes were alert for falling crumbs.

“So! Your mother and I have some news to share,” Pa announced to the four children.

Tess kicked Logan’s leg under the table. Logan kicked her back.

“What is it, Pa?” Drew asked, glancing up from his sums.

"I've decided to get a job," Pa explained. Ma squeezed his hand.

Logan was confused. What was Pa saying? He already *had* a job. He was a farmer!

"We can't make enough money growing crops," Pa went on. "Times are tough. There are lots of families giving up on their farms. But I'm hopeful that I can find work in Sherman. In fact, I have already posted several letters."

Drew frowned and returned to adding numbers.

“Oh, Pa,” said Tess. Her chin trembled.

Logan took a bite of stew. It tasted different for some reason. He couldn’t imagine not being farmers anymore. The Pryces had farmed this land since before he, Drew, Tess, and Annie were born . . . since before Pa and Ma were born.

Besides, what could Pa do in Sherman? It was nothing like Maple Ridge. It was a big city full of shops, offices, and factories. Pa couldn't till soil or sow seeds there.

Drew pointed to his notebook. "I just added up the numbers. If

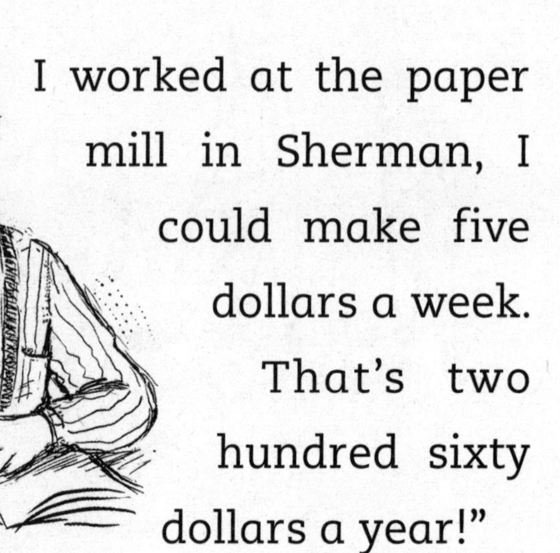

I worked at the paper mill in Sherman, I could make five dollars a week. That's two hundred sixty dollars a year!"

Pa shook his head. "You will do no such thing."

"But, Pa!" Drew protested.

"No arguments," said Pa. "It's important that you stay in school."

"I could sell my Fox-Away," Logan suggested.

"I bet I could get a dollar for it!"

"What's a Fox-Away, Lolo?" asked Annie curiously.

Logan stuck a biscuit into his mouth as he reached into his gunnysack. He pulled out the tin cup. "The Fox-Away is my latest and greatest invention. I'm almost finished with it. You hang it on the door of your henhouse to scare foxes away," he said through a mouthful of biscuit.

"No one's going to pay a dollar for your junk," Drew teased him.

"Logan's inventions are not junk!" Tess burst out.

"I'm sure someone would gladly pay a dollar for Logan's Fox-Away," said Ma quickly. "Don't you agree, Dale?"

"Absolutely, Alice," replied Pa.

Annie clutched her doll to her chest. "Do I have to sell Mrs. Wigglesworth?"

"No! No one is selling anything," declared Pa. "Thank you all for offering to help. But we're going to be fine."

Ma put her arms around Annie and Tess. "Yes. We're going to be just fine," she said brightly.

Logan took another bite of stew. He finally realized why it tasted

different. There was no meat in it—only potatoes and carrots.

Logan furrowed his brow in thought. There *had* to be a way for him to make money for his family.

But how?

DREW'S PLAN

The next morning, Logan, Tess, and Drew walked to school together. They always did so unless it was raining or snowing, in which case Pa took them in the buggy. The schoolhouse was exactly one mile from their farm. Skeeter always followed for the first quarter of a mile, until Logan convinced

him to turn around.

The walk took just about twenty minutes. School started at eight o'clock sharp. Of course, the Pryce children had been up since five o'clock to do their usual chores. These included cleaning the barn, brushing the horses, and milking the cows. Even little Annie pitched in, collecting eggs from the henhouse and helping to churn the butter.

This morning, Logan carried several logs. It was his turn to bring fire-wood to the school. He also carried his lunch pail and a new slingshot that he'd made.

As he, Tess, and Drew made their way down the muddy country road, they passed many farms and orchards. Logan noticed that some of the other farmers' fields seemed as dry and empty as their own.

Drew seemed to notice too. "You see? Everyone's giving up on

their land. It's a good thing Pa and I are applying for jobs in Sherman."

"*Pa's* applying for jobs in Sherman. He said *you* have to stay in school," Logan pointed out. One of his logs tumbled to the ground; he bent down to get it.

"I don't care what Pa says," said Drew with a shrug. "Lots of kids quit school to work. Even Uncle Archie did that, and look at him now!"

Logan mulled this over. Their uncle Archie was an important lawyer in Sherman. He, Aunt Violet, and cousins, Freddy and Clementine, lived in a fancy house. They even had maids to do their chores.

"I already have a plan," Drew went on. "I'm going to write a letter to the paper mill. I'm also going to write to Mr. Lambert. Maybe I can be an apprentice at his blacksmith shop."

"What's an ap-pren-tice?" Logan asked.

"It's when you learn a trade from someone," replied Drew.

Tess hugged her lunch pail to

her chest. "But, Drew! How are you going to travel to Sherman and back every day? We only have one buggy!"

"I have a plan for that, too. I'm going to ask Uncle Archie and Aunt Violet if I can live with them," Drew explained.

Live with Uncle Archie and Aunt Violet? Logan's jaw

dropped. If Drew lived with them, he would have his own bedroom. He would have maids to do his chores for him. He would eat meat every day.

Not fair! Logan thought, his fists clenching. This time, *all* the logs tumbled to the ground.

AT SCHOOL

The Maple Ridge School was a small red building that sat on a gentle, sloping hill. Behind it were grassy fields for playing, trees for climbing, and a garden for growing fruits and vegetables. Some days, the children picked turnips and carrots to add to their soup for lunch.

Smoke curled out of the chimney as Logan, Tess, Drew, and the other students hurried into the one-room schoolhouse. Logan set his lunch pail on top of the stove to keep his stew warm for later and put his logs in a copper bin.

He then took a seat at his desk. The boys sat on one side and the girls sat on the other. The youngest children sat up front and the oldest children sat in the back.

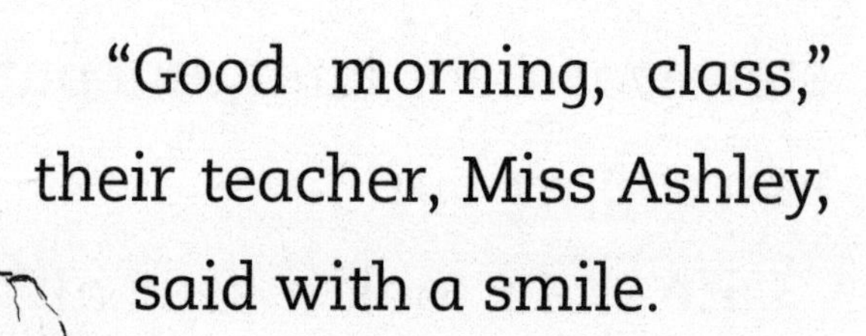

"Good morning, class," their teacher, Miss Ashley, said with a smile.

"Good morning, Miss Ashley!" the students replied in unison.

Miss Ashley was young and pretty. She had her blond hair in a bun and wore a blue shawl the color of cornflowers.

As always, she started the day

with roll call. She read the students' names from a list to make sure that they were present. After roll call, she moved on to reading.

"Tess, will you come up front and recite our poem for today?" Miss Ashley asked. "It is on page twenty-nine of your readers," she added to the rest of the class.

Tess rose from her desk and walked eagerly to the front of the room. She could be shy at times, but she was never shy about reciting.

Tess opened her reader, which was a book full of poems, stories, and essays. She cleared her throat and began to speak in a fine, clear voice:

After reading came writing and spelling. Miss Ashley wrote some words on the blackboard, and the students copied them on small slates. The room filled with the loud sound of stone pens scratching against stone tablets as everyone worked. The pale sun shone

through the windows and provided the only light to see by.

After writing and spelling came morning recess. Outside, Logan dug through his pockets for a twig that he'd carved into a whistle. He had just started to play the song "Polly Wolly Doodle" on it when his friend

Anthony Bruna ran up to him.

"Logan!" said Anthony, brushing a stray black curl out of his eyes. "Do you want to trade marbles?"

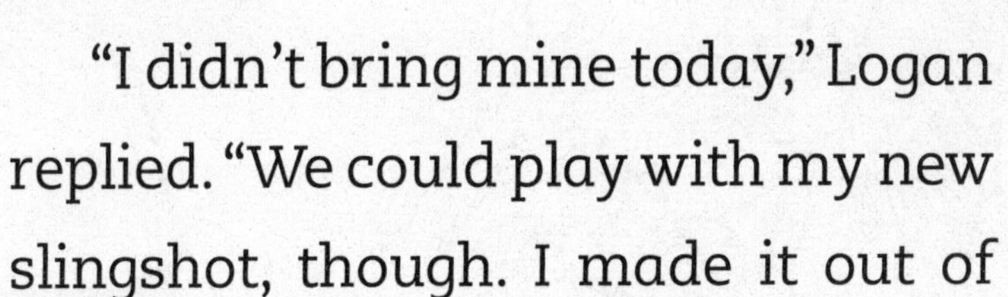

"I didn't bring mine today," Logan replied. "We could play with my new slingshot, though. I made it out of

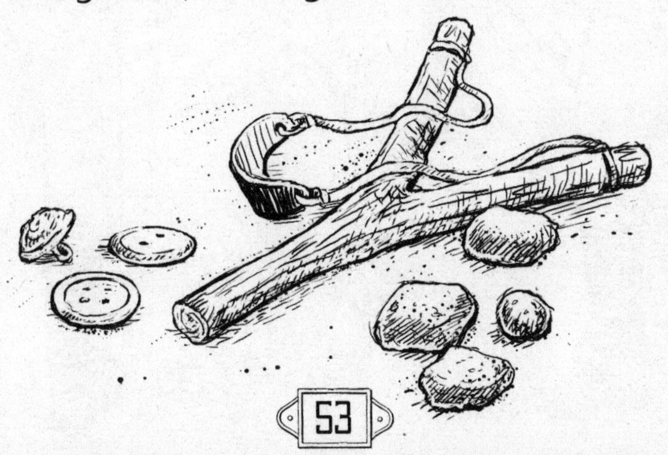

rubber tubing and a maple branch."

"Swell!"

As the two boys took turns pitching pebbles against a tree, Logan told Anthony about his family's news.

"So it looks like Pa's not going to be a farmer anymore," Logan finished.

"Gosh, that's too bad," Anthony said, shaking his head. "You really are very lucky, though. At least your pa's home. Mine has to go to Sherman every day for his job at the steel mill. He has to leave at five every morning and doesn't come home until late. Most nights, he's so tired that he goes straight to bed without his supper."

"Oh, sorry," said Logan. "I didn't know that."

And then Logan thought of something. It was something that made his stomach hurt.

What if Pa got a job like Mr. Bruna's? Logan and the rest of the family would never see him!

PA'S NEW JOB

"I got a job!" Pa announced when Logan, Tess, and Drew came home from school the following day.

Ma glanced up from a tub of soapy water and smiled happily at the children. Tuesday was laundry day. Wet shirts and dresses hung on lines that stretched across the kitchen. Annie sat on the floor playing with clothespins. Skeeter rested in front of the stove.

"Wow, Pa! You got a job so soon?" asked Drew, surprised. "Didn't you just post your letters to Sherman?"

"This job isn't in Sherman. It's right here in Maple Ridge. And it's only for a few days,"

Pa explained. "Mayberry's General Store received a large shipment of goods from Chicago. Mrs. Mayberry needs my help unpacking the boxes. I start tomorrow morning. By this weekend, we'll be five dollars richer!"

"Hooray!" Tess shouted, hugging Pa.

"Hooray!" Annie echoed, hugging Mrs. Wigglesworth.

Suddenly, everyone was in a good mood.

To celebrate, Ma baked a ginger cake. She served it with dollops of thick cream that she had skimmed from a pitcher of milk.

As they ate, Pa spoke some more about the job.

"Mrs. Mayberry told me that this is a very large shipment. In fact, she said she is even looking for a second person to help," he explained.

"I wish that could be me, Pa! But I already promised Miss Ashley I would do chores around the schoolhouse," Drew said.

Logan quickly sat up in his chair. "What about me?"

Pa was confused. "What *about* you?"

"I could help out with the shipment!" replied Logan.

Pa rubbed his whiskers. Ma caught his eye and nodded.

"Hmm. All right. I'll speak to Mrs. Mayberry tomorrow morning," Pa said to Logan. "Why don't you come by the store after school? If Mrs. Mayberry says yes, you can stay and help me with the shipment. You can help me on Thursday and Friday, too. The pay is a dollar."

A *dollar?* Logan grinned at Tess, and she grinned back. A dollar was a lot of money!

"You will have to work hard and do as I say," Pa went on. "Nothing can go wrong. Do you understand?"

"Yes, Pa!" said Logan, nodding.

Logan couldn't stop grinning as

he dug into his cake. He'd wanted to make money for his family, and now he had the chance. It wasn't exactly a fancy job in Sherman, but it was a start!

MAYBERRY'S GENERAL STORE
DRY GOODS ~ GROCERIES ~ CLOTHING
GENERAL MERCHANDISE

THE GENERAL STORE

On Wednesday after school, Logan walked over to Mayberry's. The sign in front read:

Mayberry's was on Main Street in downtown Maple Ridge. The other buildings on the street included a barbershop, a church, and the town hall. Horses hitched to posts grazed lazily on oats. Other horses trotted along, making *clip-clop* sounds as

they pulled carts behind them.

Logan had always loved the general store. On Saturdays, Ma went there to trade her homemade

butter and jam for tea, sugar, and other items she needed. Logan, Tess, and Annie liked to come along because Mrs. Mayberry sometimes gave them penny candies.

Mayberry's also sold other goods, like clothing, medicine, and books. In fact, even though Logan's boots had been hand-me-downs from Drew, they were originally from there. Last year, Tess had used her Christmas money to buy *The Adventures of Huckleberry Finn* by Mr. Mark Twain.

CLOSED
FLOUR

A tiny bell jingled as Logan opened the front door. The air inside the store smelled like spices, coffee, and kerosene oil.

"Well, hello there, young man!" Mrs. Mayberry stood behind the counter, weighing bags of flour. "Your father tells me you'd like to help out this week. I told him that was fine by me. Why don't you get started? He's in the back unpacking boxes."

"Thanks, Mrs. Mayberry!" Logan said excitedly.

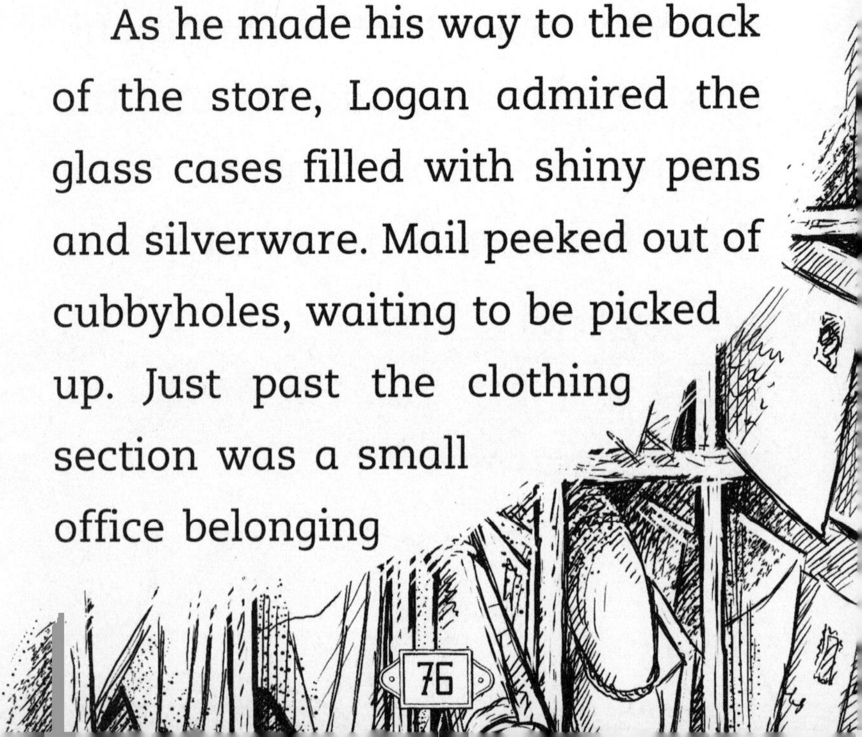

As he made his way to the back of the store, Logan admired the glass cases filled with shiny pens and silverware. Mail peeked out of cubbyholes, waiting to be picked up. Just past the clothing section was a small office belonging

to Mr. Mayberry. According to Pa, he was away on a trip to buy new goods for the store.

Logan found Pa crouching beside a large pile of boxes. Pa glanced up and wiped his brow with the back of his sleeve. "Hello, son! I'm glad you're here."

"What can I do, Pa?" asked Logan.

"First, we unload the items from these boxes. Then we check off each item on this list." Pa held up a bundle of papers. "Once the item is checked off, we can put it on the shelves, where it will be ready for customers to buy."

"Got it!" said Logan.

The two of them worked steadily for the next hour. Logan quickly learned where everything went in the store.

At one point, Mrs. Mayberry called Pa up front to help a customer with a heavy crate. "Don't

do anything until I get back," Pa told Logan.

"I won't," Logan promised.

While Pa helped the customer, Logan leaned against a crate and waited. After a while, he noticed a small box sitting by itself in the corner.

M. BIRD was written across it. *Maybe I could tackle that one on my own,* he thought. *Pa would probably be glad to have one less box to deal with.*

Logan opened the box and peered at the contents. Inside were three pairs of women's gloves, a

silk hat, and a dozen hairpins. He pulled out the items and placed them on the correct shelves throughout the store. The entire task took less than five minutes.

Easy as pie, Logan thought with a smile. At this rate, he and Pa would be finished with the shipment in no time at all!

THE BIG MIX-UP

"Logan did a fine job today at Mayberry's," declared Pa when he and Logan got home.

Tess and Drew sat at the table doing schoolwork. Ma heated water on the stove for Annie's bath. Skeeter gnawed on an old beef bone.

"I knew he would!" Ma said, drying her hands on her apron.

"What exactly did you two men have to do?"

"Lots!" Logan pushed back his shoulders and ran a hand through his scruffy blond hair. He liked that Ma had called him and Pa "men." "I even unpacked a box all by myself," he added proudly.

Pa frowned. "What box are you talking about, son?"

"While you were up front, I unpacked one of the boxes and put everything on the shelves," Logan

replied. "The box was in the corner. It had something to do with a bird."

Pa turned pale. "You mean . . . the box marked M. BIRD?"

Logan nodded. "That's the one!"

"What's wrong, Dale?" Ma asked worriedly.

"That box was different from the others. We weren't supposed to unpack it," Pa explained. "It's for Mr. Bird. He ordered some special items from Chicago for his wife's birthday. He's planning on picking up the box in person tomorrow."

"*What?*" Logan gasped.

Pa peered at his pocket watch. "I'd better get down to the store right away. I need to find those items and return

them to Mr. Bird's box. Otherwise, someone might buy them by mistake!"

Logan's lip quivered. "I'm sorry, Pa. I was just . . ."

. . . *trying to help*, he wanted to say. But before he could finish his sentence, Pa grabbed his overcoat and ran out the door.

MAKING IT RIGHT

Logan sat on his bed, turning his Fox-Away over and over on his lap. It was a dumb invention. He was a dumb inventor. *He* was dumb—plain and simple.

How could he have messed things up so badly at the general store?

In the other bed, Drew leafed

through *Popular Science* magazine by lamplight. The two boys shared a small room in the back of the house. It was right above the kitchen, so it was warm and toasty even on chilly nights.

Skeeter lay on the rug and

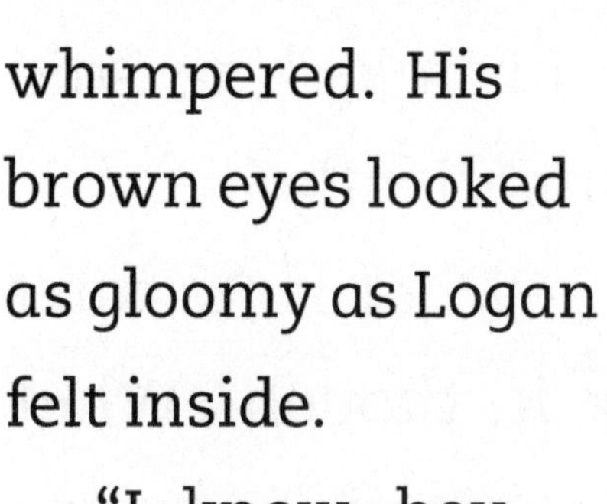

whimpered. His brown eyes looked as gloomy as Logan felt inside.

"I know, boy. My life is ruined," Logan murmured.

Drew set his magazine down with a sigh. "Your life isn't ruined. You just made

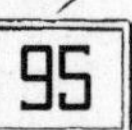

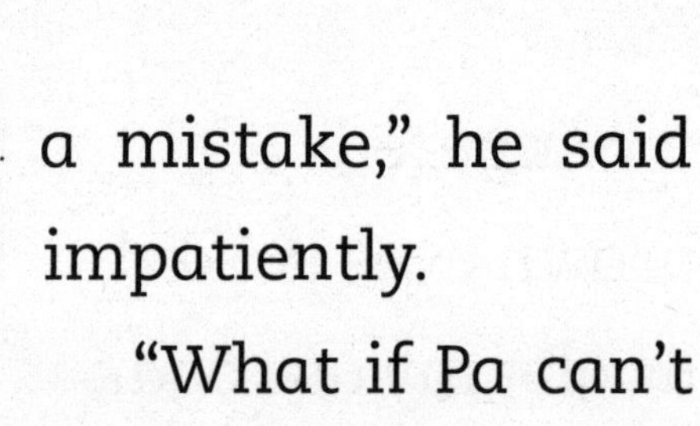

a mistake," he said impatiently.

"What if Pa can't fix it, though? What if someone already bought Mrs. Bird's birthday presents? What if Mrs. Mayberry finds out it was my fault? What if Pa doesn't get paid because of me? What if Pa never finds work again?" Logan put his hands over his eyes.

"Stop being so dramatic," said Drew.

"What's dra-mat-ic?"

"It's when you make a big deal out of something that's not a big deal."

Someone knocked quietly on the door. Tess poked her head into the room. "May we come in?"

Before the boys could answer, Annie

skipped inside, with Tess trailing behind. Both girls were dressed in flannel nightshirts. Dozens of cotton-rag ribbons covered Annie's head.

“Tessie is curling my hair!” Annie said happily. “*And* we brought you presents!” She thrust a shiny marble at Logan.

Tess handed him a comb with missing teeth. “I thought you could use this in your Fix-It Shop.”

“Thanks. But why are you guys giving me presents?” Logan asked, confused.

“’Cause we wanted to cheer you up!” Annie explained.

“Hey, I need some cheering up too,” Drew joked. “Where are *my* presents?”

Footsteps sounded on the stairs. A moment later, Pa and Ma came into the boys’ room.

Pa was still wearing his over-coat, and his cheeks were red from the cold night air.

"Good news!" Pa announced. "I got to Mayberry's in time."

Logan bolted up in his bed. "You did?"

Pa nodded. "Mrs. Bird's birthday

presents were still on the shelves. I was able to return them to their box and seal everything up."

"Was Mrs. Mayberry mad?" Logan asked nervously.

Pa shook his head. "She wasn't mad at all. She knows it was an honest mistake."

"Next time, just do as your father says and don't get any fancy ideas," Ma told Logan.

"Yes, Ma! And thank you, Pa!" said Logan.

"You're welcome, son."

Pa smiled at Logan. So did Ma and Tess. Annie climbed up on his bed and nestled her head

on his shoulder. Drew gave him a thumbs-up sign and returned to his magazine. Skeeter wagged his tail.

Logan felt all the worry whoosh out of his chest. Everything was right and normal again.

And for the next few days at the general store, he would do exactly as Pa said. He could always save his fancy ideas for the Fix-It Shop!

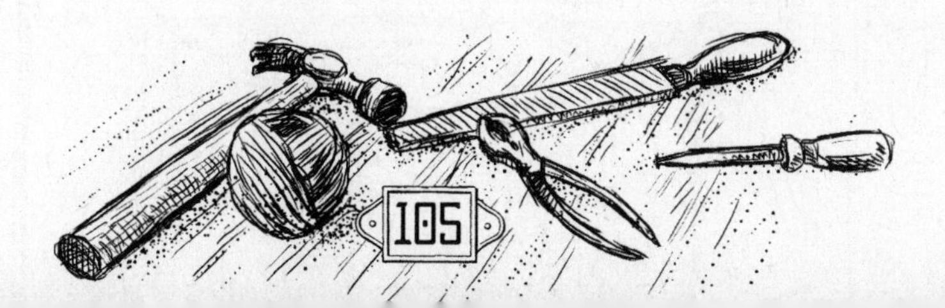

THE MAPLE SYRUP PARTY

Sunday was bright and cool as everyone gathered at the Pryce farm for their annual sugaring off.

Logan and Tess stood in the doorway of the sugarhouse, licking syrup from their fingers. They loved maple syrup parties. Inside, the Brunas, Mrs. Mayberry, and other friends and neighbors boiled sap

that they had collected from maple trees. Platters of baked beans, ham, pancakes, and apple pie covered a long table.

Outside, the woods glistened with melting snow. A cardinal landed on a branch and shook drops of water from its red wings.

Children ran around or poured hot syrup on snow to make jack wax candy.

Logan breathed in the delicious maple-scented air. "I wish we could have a sugaring off every day!" he said to Tess.

"Do you think this will be our last one?" asked Tess with a sad smile.

"No," Logan replied. "Just because Pa's not going to farm anymore doesn't mean we're going to stop making food. We'll still need syrup and milk and butter and vegetables

and eggs. . . ." His face lit up. "*Eggs!*"

"Eggs? What about them?"

"Come with me. I have to show you something!"

Logan started running through the woods. Tess followed, and so did Skeeter. When they got to the henhouse, Logan stopped.

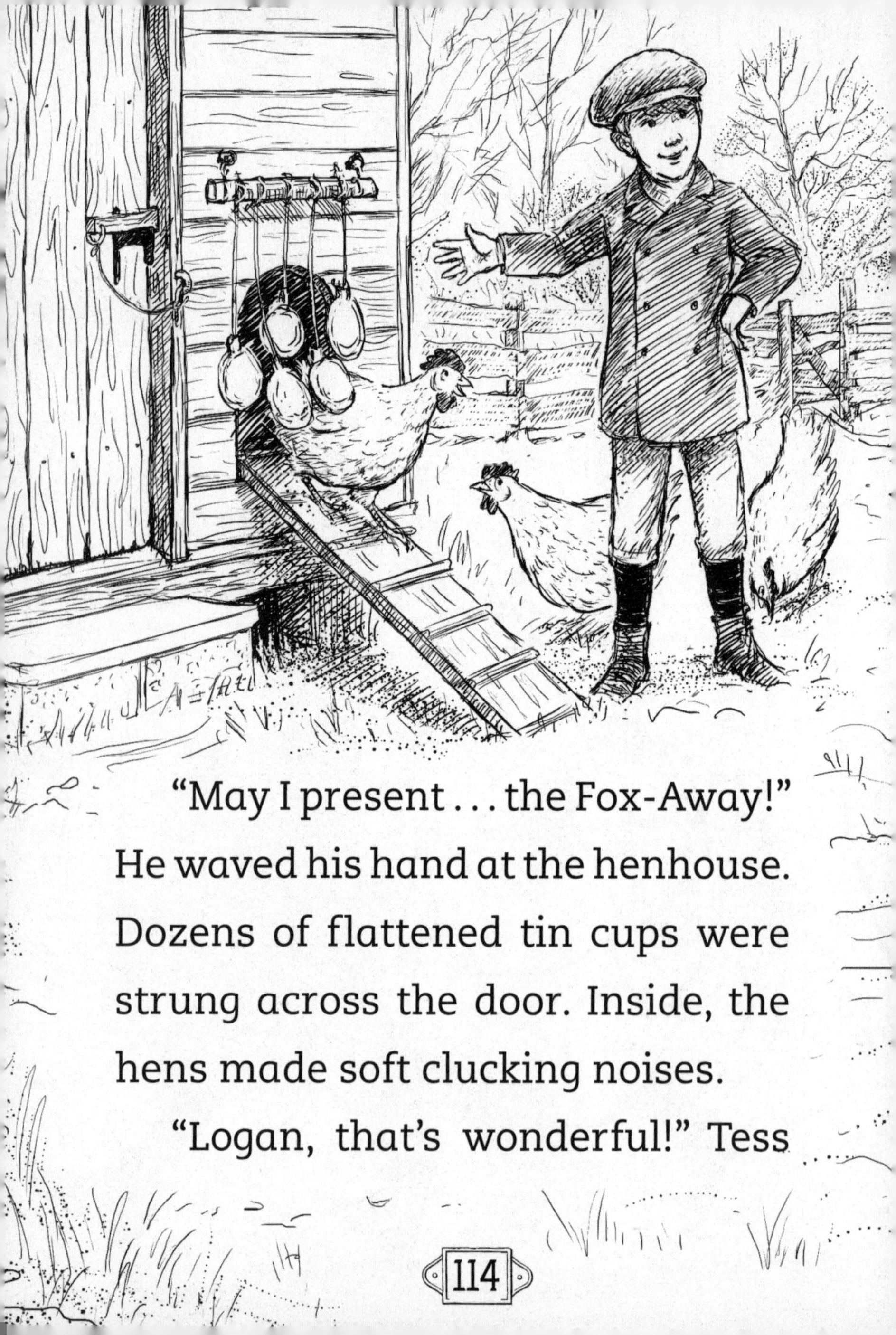

"May I present . . . the Fox-Away!" He waved his hand at the henhouse. Dozens of flattened tin cups were strung across the door. Inside, the hens made soft clucking noises.

"Logan, that's wonderful!" Tess

cried out. "When did you finish it?"

"This morning. I put it up just after breakfast. The loud clanking from the Fox-Away will scare the foxes so that the hens can lay their eggs in peace," Logan explained.

"I think this could be your best invention yet," Tess told him.

Skeeter barked in agreement.

As they stood there admiring the Fox-Away, Logan thought about his family's farm. He wasn't sure what would happen to it tomorrow . . . or in the next month . . . or in the next year.

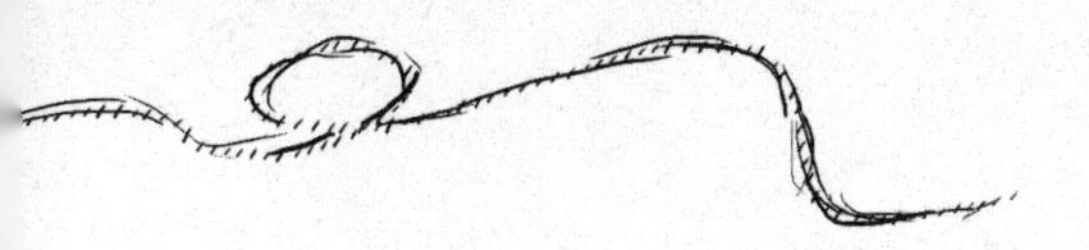

Would Pa ever go back to planting wheat? Would they have to move away some day?

Logan *was* sure about a few things, though. No matter what happened, he would go on fixing and

inventing things. Tess would go on reading books and being smart. Drew would go on making big plans for his future. Annie would go on being sweet, adorable Annie.

And no matter what, their family would go on being a family. As far as Logan was concerned, that was the best thing of all!

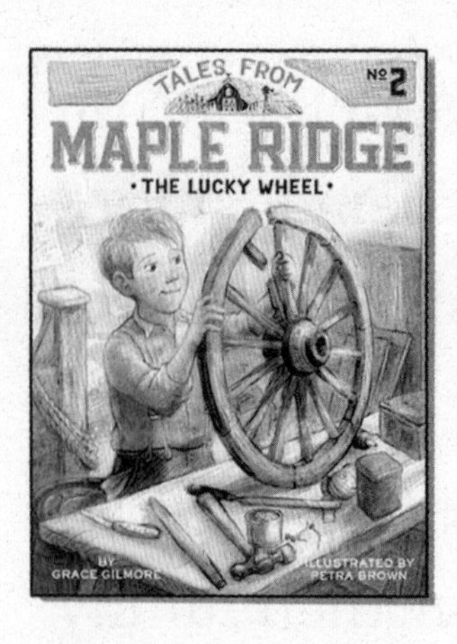

Check out the next

TALES FROM MAPLE RIDGE

adventure!

HERE'S A SNEAK PEEK!

The next morning, Logan woke up earlier than usual.

It was pitch black outside as he headed to the barn. A sliver of moon lingered in the sky. The air was clear and cold, and he could see his breath.

Skeeter trotted along beside him, alert for raccoons and opossums.

In the barn, Logan raced through his usual chores. First, he milked the cows. Next, he brushed the horses, Lightning and Buttercup, and mucked their stalls, too.

When his chores were done, he got to work in his Fix-It Shop. The shop took up one corner of the barn. A worktable, a chair, and some crates were its only furniture.

The broken wheel sat in the middle of Logan's worktable. He picked it up and studied it.

He had a plan.

Find excerpts, activities, and more at
TalesfromMapleRidge.com!